D1386391

THIS WALKER BOOK BELONGS TO:

_____

_____

_____

_____

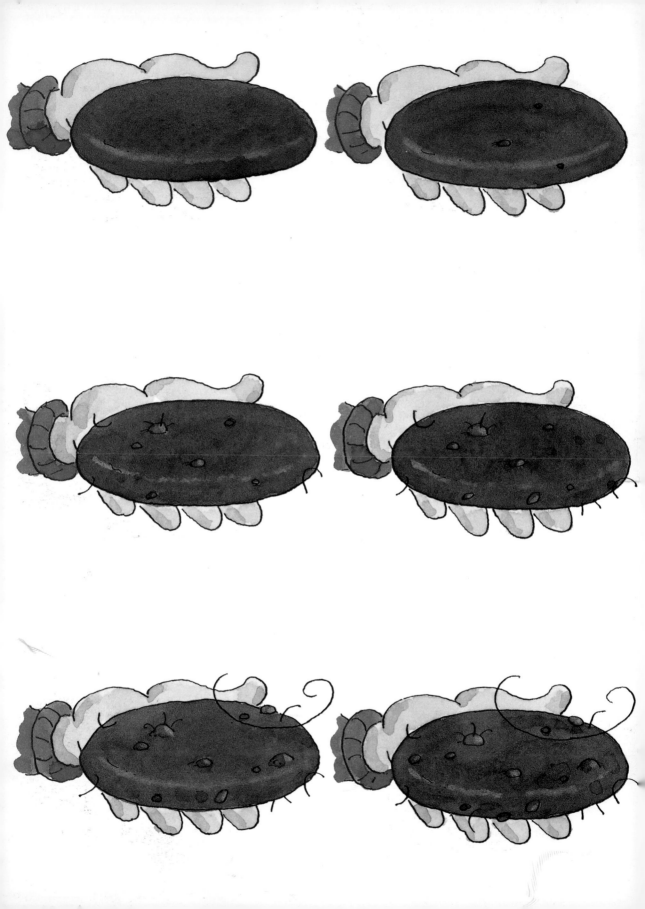

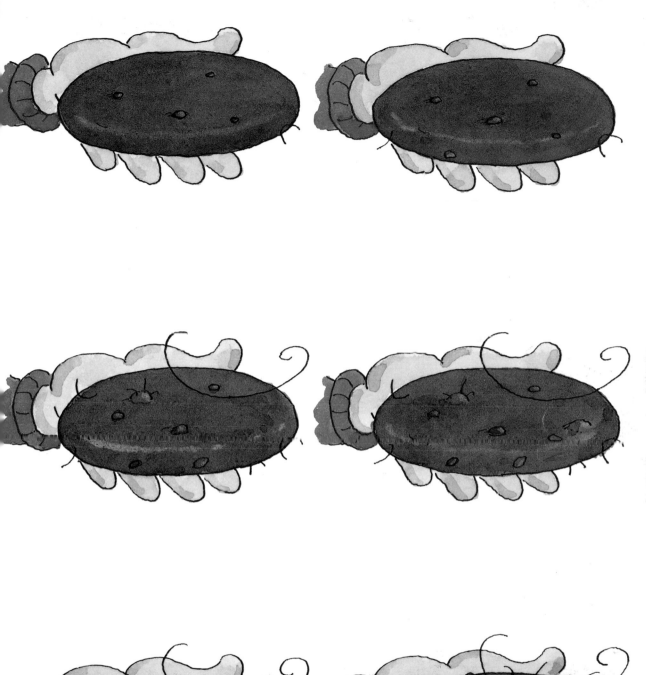

To Michael and Patrick,
who have to fight their mother
for the last chocolate biscuit. . .
J.R.

To Matthew
A.R.

First published in Great Britain 2000
by Walker Books Ltd
87 Vauxhall Walk
London SE11 5HJ

2 4 6 8 10 9 7 5 3 1

Text © 1997 Jamie Rix
Illustrations © 1997 Arthur Robins

This book has been typeset in Beniolo.

Printed in Hong Kong

British Library Cataloguing in Publication Data
A catalogue record for this book is
available from the British Library.

ISBN 0-7445-7813-2

The Last Chocolate Biscuit

Written by
Jamie Rix

Illustrated by
Arthur Robins

WALKER BOOKS
AND SUBSIDIARIES
LONDON • BOSTON • SYDNEY

There was one chocolate biscuit left
and it was shouting,
"Maurice, eat me!"
So I leaned across the table
to do as I was told.

"Maurice!" gasped my mother.
"Where are your manners?
Offer it to everyone else first."
"*Everyone else?*" I said.
"*Everyone else,*" she insisted.

So **I** carried the last chocolate biscuit around in my pocket for the next six weeks and did as **I** was told.
I offered it to

my brother,

my father,

my nan,

and the cat ... but they didn't want it.

I offered it to

the papergirl,

the postman,

my teacher,

and a dinner lady . . .

but they didn't want it.

I took a train to the city and offered it to

a window cleaner,

a bus driver,

a business man,

and a stone lion . . .

but they didn't want it.

I went all round the world and
offered it to Presidents
and Kings . . .

So I took the last chocolate biscuit into space and offered it to a space monster. But the space monster didn't want the chocolate biscuit. . .

He wanted me!

"Maurice Monster!" gasped his monster mother. "Where are your manners? Offer the human being to everyone else first."

"*Everyone else?*" he said.
"*Everyone else,*" she insisted.

So he carried me around in his pocket for the next six weeks and did as he was told. He offered me to

his brottleswat,   his fatter,

his nench,

and the cattapurch . . . but they didn't want me.

He offered me to

the pamplemoy,

the sackforth,

the dillyco,   and his cybernetic expositor . . .

but they didn't want me.

He took a shuttle to **Mars** and offered me to

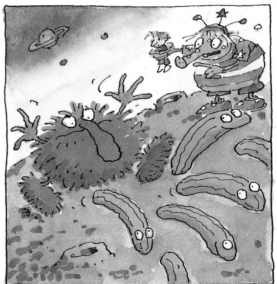

a mickleman,   a stork-rauncher,

a petrified gork, and a cumber-catcher . . .

but they didn't want me.

He flew around the universe offering
me to Startling Commanders and
Hairy Wingos . . .

but they didn't want me.

So he took me back to Earth and
offered me to my mother.
"It's nice to see a space monster
with such lovely manners," she said.
"I'll be pleased to have him."

I told my mother that I'd offered the
last chocolate biscuit to everyone else,
but nobody had wanted it.
"Then you can eat it," she said. "It will
taste twice as delicious now that you've
been so polite."

I was dribbling. I'd waited a long time
to eat the last chocolate biscuit.

I took a bite. . .

It tasted like cardboard gunk-gloop with hairs on!

Do *you* want the last chocolate biscuit?

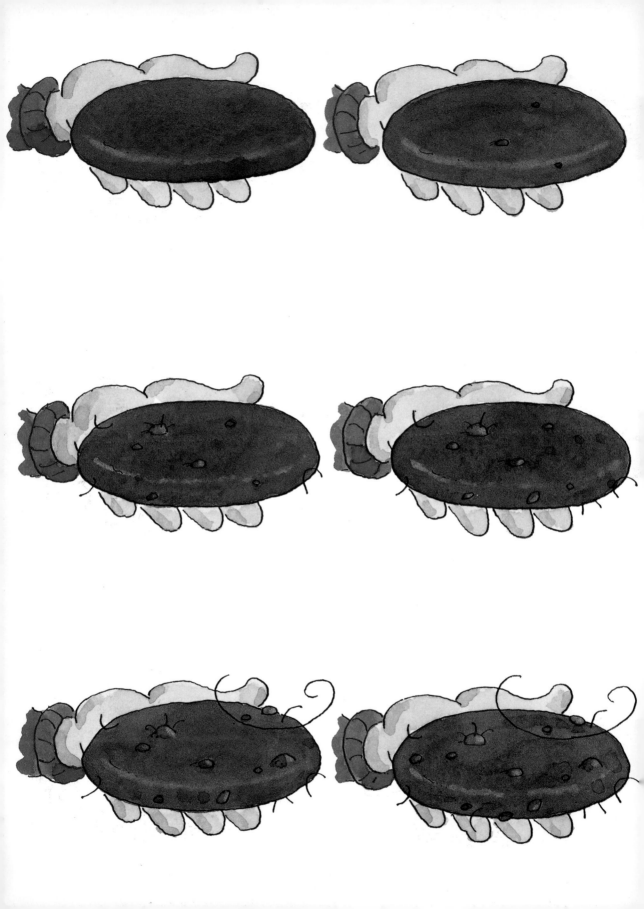

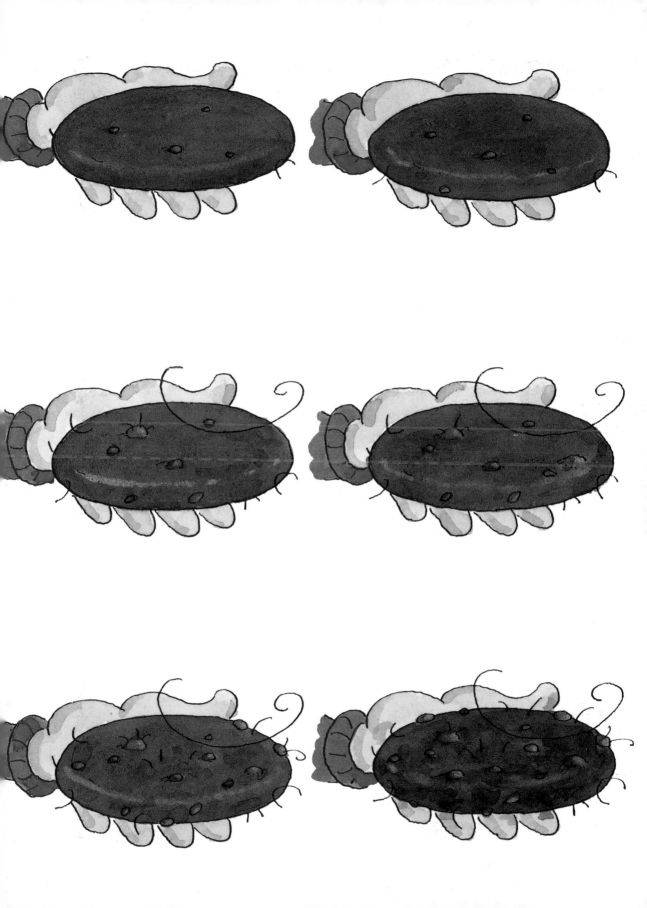

The Last Chocolate Biscuit

JAMIE RIX says of *The Last Chocolate Biscuit*, "Once, I was at a birthday party and there were three chocolate biscuits left on a plate. I could see that the boy sitting in front of the plate loved chocolate biscuits. He checked to see who was looking. Then he picked up one in his left hand and picked up one in his right hand. Only then did he realize that there was still one left on the plate. Undaunted, he leant forward and picked up the last chocolate biscuit in his mouth. Now he was stuck, he didn't have a hand left to eat them with!"

As well as writing, directing and producing shows for television, Jamie Rix is a prolific writer of children's books. His many titles include *Johnny Casanova*, *The Changing Face of Johnny Casanova* and *Free the Whales*. His book of short stories, *Grizzly Tales for Gruesome Kids* was the Children's Choice Winner for the 1990 Smarties Book Prize and has been turned into a hit television series. Jamie lives in south London with his wife Helen and sons Ben and Jack.

ARTHUR ROBINS says, "My last chocolate biscuit – the tastiest one in the packet, and even if I keep it safe in my hanky and blow off all the pocket fluff, and polish it on my sleeve, I have found people are just too polite to take it... So don't worry about offering yours around!"

Arthur Robins has worked as a freelance designer in the advertising industry, and as an illustrator for various magazines. His work has been exhibited in both London and New York. He has also illustrated numerous picture books and fiction titles for children, including *The Magic Bicycle*, *Little Rabbit Foo Foo*, *The Teeny Tiny Woman*, *Mission Ziffoid*, *The Finger-eater* and *The Magic Boathouse*. Arthur lives in Cranleigh, Surrey, with his family.

ISBN 0-7445-3651-0 (pb)

ISBN 0-7445-6942-7 (pb)

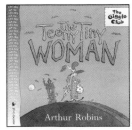

ISBN 0-7445-6022-5 (pb)

ISBN 0-7445-6945-1 (pb)

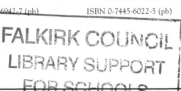